DAVIDE CALI ★ SERGE BLOCH

George
AND HIS
SHADOW

HARPER
An Imprint of HarperCollins Publishers

George and His Shadow

Text copyright © 2017 by Davide Cali

Illustrations copyright © 2017 Serge Bloch

Translated from Italian by Debbie Bibo.

www.harpercollinschildrens.com

ISBN 978-0-06-256830-4

The artist used his brain, his hands, and his computer to create the illustrations for this book.

Typography by Amy Ryan

17 18 19 20 21 SCP 10 9 8 7 6 5 4 3 2 1

❖

First Edition

It seemed like an ordinary day.

A day just like any other.

But when George woke up . . .

and went into the kitchen . . .

"Who are you?" asked George.

"I'm your shadow," answered the shadow.

"What are you doing here? Shouldn't you be on the floor?"

"I was hungry."

After breakfast George went out for a walk
and the shadow followed him.

"Perhaps you should go back to being stuck
on the ground," suggested George.

"I feel like seeing the city."

The shadow followed him everywhere that day.

George began to feel more and more annoyed.

"You know," George said, "I think it's time for you to go back to being a shadow."

The shadow didn't even answer.

So George thought about how he could make his shadow disappear.

He tried cutting him into tiny pieces.

But that didn't work.

He tried to wash him away.

But that didn't work either.

Vacuum cleaner?

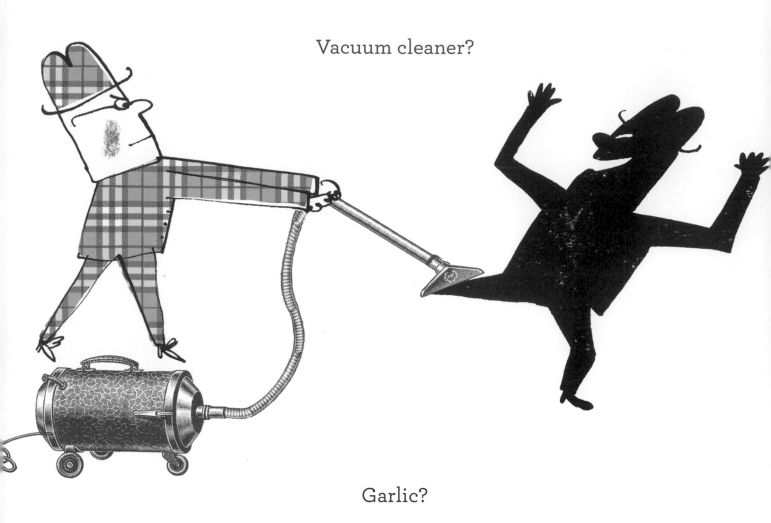

Garlic?

"Go Scooter, go!"

"Scooter?"

If Scooter didn't mind, maybe the shadow wasn't too bad.

Anyway, the shadow kind of kept them company.

And there are many things that you can do together
that you can't do alone.

Play baseball.

Or hide-and-seek.

Play cops and robbers.

Have an ice-cream eating contest.

Make a bigger splash.

"I think I'm going to take a nap,"
said the shadow after hours of playing,
and he disappeared.

Suddenly, George felt lonely.

Then came another day.

It seemed like an ordinary day.
A day just like any other.

But when George woke up and went
to the bathroom . . .

"And who are you?" asked George.

"I'm your reflection."